GAGE THE FLYING WHIPPET

By Darla Desiderio

Book One in the Gage the Flying Whippet Series

Acknowledgement

For my Father, who inspired me to dream big dreams.

To Grant Mahan, Cover Art, Artist & Student,
Rhode Island School of Design.

Bree Stallings, Chapter Illustrations, Artist, Teacher of Youth.

TABLE OF CONTENTS

PREFACE

I was inspired to write this book for many awesome reasons, including my love of dogs and my belief in the potential that all kids possess.

My love for my dog, Gage, stands out the most. His facial expressions communicate his every emotion. When Gage looks into my face with his beautiful eyes, shaped like perfect jewels, I can feel his warm dog hug.

I giggle at the mischievous expression that creeps onto his face when he wants to play. His ears lie flat, and the edges of his mouth furl up before he spins around like a toy top, smiling at his own silliness.

I love Gage because he curls up next to me like a cat and tucks his soft fur into my body while drifting off to dog sleep, comforted by my affection for him.

Gage is a White Brindle Whippet. He was destined to be a show dog before it was discovered he was too small to perform in the ring. It sounds like a sad story, but Gage doesn't know he's too small to be a proper Whippet.
He's big on Whippet personality!

CHAPTER 1: Sammie for Short

Samantha is my name, or Sammie for short. I'm not the most popular kid in class, but I have some girls that are my close friends. I'm petite and weigh 98 pounds soaking wet, as my dad describes me.

My mom says I'm too sensitive, which I don't get. If she knew about what I could imagine in my head, she'd be surprised! I love sports, and I'm a really good athlete, but being a great student is reserved for other kids. School was always hard, and the seventh grade was especially difficult for me. I felt different 24/7, and it made me tired. The seventh grade was almost over, thank God.

"Sammie," Mr. Danner said, "come sit up here and read this passage from *A Catcher in the Rye*." Of course, reading out loud was like climbing a mountain for me. I did my best to begin, but it was slow going. Not known for his patience, Mr. D snatched the book from me and read the passage.

"See," he said, "it's easy!" I thought at that moment I understood why the main character was so unhappy. I finished the book on my own and understood it. I could memorize anything and comprehend as well as any kid my age, but reading out loud was just hard. Perhaps the fact that I didn't do so well wasn't as bad compared to the fact that Mr. D was missing a sensitivity chip!

Math was tougher than English. Numbers were like scrambled eggs. I overheard Mr. Rodriguez wonder how my Algebra class would ever make it in the real world. Truth is, I wondered, too. I would never share with anyone that I, like Mr. Rodriguez, worried about where I would end up in the world.

The school year was coming to an end, so my homeroom teacher tried to distract us from the anticipation of summertime by concocting some thoughtful games.

This morning she went around the room and asked each student what type of animal they would be if they were able to choose. Charley said a horse, and Nancy thought a cat would be nice. She stopped at my desk, and I hesitated. The realization came before the words. "I want to be a bird of prey,"

I said excitedly. What? Everyone was like, "Why do you want to be a buzzard?"

"No," I said, "I want to be an eagle."

After the last student contributed to the game, I realized I was the only bird girl in the bunch. The thought occupied my mind the rest of the day. It didn't matter if I daydreamed in Math because I didn't understand most of it anyway, so I just sat in a dream state thinking about why I wanted to be an eagle. I wasn't really sure; I just knew it was an exciting idea.

"Why an eagle?" I thought to myself. "I know why," I whispered in my head. Sounds from class came and went as I saw the eagle in my mind's eye. Soaring in the sky, passing the sun over a beautiful landscape of mountains and tall trees, the eagle was searching for food. It surveyed the earth, looking for a rabbit or small animal to bring back to its fledglings. Now, I wanted someone to ask me what my secret was. I thought they would be so amazed if they knew, but nobody did, which was fine because it was my secret. I wanted to fly...

CHAPTER 2: Home Free

I realized I had forgotten my yo-yo. Nancy said she would ask the bus driver to wait for me, so I jumped down from the first step of the school bus and landed on the pavement. I ran through the front double doors of the school, turned right, and burst open the doors to the stairway leading to the seventh and eight grade level. Mr. D'Angelo, the vice principal, yelled down at me, "Young man, slow down! It may be the last day of school, but that is no excuse to run!" I was on the last step when I looked up at him. "Oh," he said. "No running."

"Great," I thought to myself as I found the yo-yo on the top shelf of my locker, "I look like a boy." I took my ponytail out of my baseball cap and ran back to the bus.

The torture was over, school ended, and I was back in my element! Swimming in our pool and setting off on bike adventures with my best friend Nancy made the summer great. We were gone all day and would return before dusk so our moms wouldn't worry. The acres in back of our home were my sanctuary. I loved to create fantasies where I was supreme! In them, I showed off my knowledge of bushes, trees, bugs, and birds for my imaginary friends. I was a Native American. I was an Olympic long jumper. When I was riding my dirt bike, I was the first girl dirt bike jumping champion! I accepted my award perched on top of a dirt mound, apologizing to the boys for being such a talented girl rider.

When mom sat me down on Sunday and said "summer school," I didn't say much. After all, I deserved to be punished. I was a terrible student. Just ask the vice principal. It was kids like me who weren't candidates for vocational school yet were unable to deliver good grades, which threw off his average of college-bound students. "What a stupid failure I am," I thought to myself.

I overheard my mother on the phone listening to the results of my IQ test, and much to my parents' relief I had an above-average IQ. Yippee! Little good it did me. None of my friends were going to summer school. It was reserved for me, the girl who wanted to be an eagle.

Of course, for the rest of the day I retreated to the woods, making up some fantasy that was much better than the idea of walking into remedial math class. The sun was setting, and I knew my mom would have an amazing meal for the family waiting inside the house. My mom was a great cook. I ran full tilt down the path out of the woods and into the front door, where I saw a magnificent meal of pasta, grilled veggies, fresh bread, and cheese. The bread and cheese was delivered that morning by my grandparents. "Mom, this is awesome!" I said with a smile.

I brought my plate into the kitchen and helped my older sister clean up after dinner. "Does anyone want to go to Mr. Jackson's store for candy?" my dad said enthusiastically. I whipped around the corner from the kitchen and into the breakfast room where my dad sat at the end of the dinner table. The breakfast room was where we ate our casual dinners. The dining room was reserved for formal occasions.

"I want to go, Dad!"

"Let's go, kid!" he said. I dashed out the door and slid into the passenger seat, crashing up against the driver's side door. I scooted back into the passenger seat and waited for Dad to get behind the wheel. My dad's Cadillac was banana colored, and it had a lime-green top. Mom said the color was nauseating, but Dad thought it was funny. Dad would always say to us while driving in the "Tank," as we called it, "We don't have to worry about anything when we're behind the wheel of the Tank! We're invincible, kids!"

Dad maneuvered the Tank down our driveway and through the iron gates. The wrought-iron gates were each mounted onto a stone pillar. The gates were permanently opened, welcoming anyone who wanted to visit or who wandered through because they lost their way driving around the mountain roads. Dad pressed on the brake at the end of the driveway and came to a soft stop just as the wheels of the Tank eased back up over the dip at the end. We lived on the corner, so we had to do what my Dad called the "triple check." He whipped his head up and down Claremont Road and then over his right shoulder down Post Lane. Dad would then say, "Clear!" before he pulled out. It always made me giggle.

"Look out, Sammie. Here comes Mrs. Poole!" Dad said.

"Wow, Dad, she's flying!" I said. Mrs. Poole drove a metallic-gray convertible and always pushed the pedal to the floor. The local policeman commented to my mom that they had clocked Mrs. Poole going 75 miles per hour up the mountain, which has a speed limit of only 35. Mrs. Poole wore her gray-streaked hair in a tight bun pulled away from her slender face. She never beeped at us or waved like I noticed other people did. After she zoomed past us, my dad pulled out, laughing.

"Sammie, she drives so fast I don't know how her bun doesn't fly off her head!" As we drove down the mountain, I balanced on one knee to see Mrs. Poole's brake lights in the Cadillac's rearview mirror. As she made a sharp right into her driveway, Mingpoo, her Pekingese's head, peered over her bony shoulder. Mom always said that nothing much mattered to Mrs. Poole other than her precious dog Mingpoo.

My dad and I drove down the mountain to the candy store. Driving in the big Tank, we floated down the mountain. The Tank rolled over each gentle hill until we turned into the gravel driveway of Jackson's Candy Shop.

"Dad," I asked, as I used my whole weight to shut the

heavy car door, "does Mrs. Poole not wave because all she cares about is Mingpoo?"

"No, Sammie. She doesn't wave because she's, well, a wealthy woman from an old-money family, and we're the first people of Italian descent to move up toward the mountain." I thought about what Dad said, and he was right. All the other Italian kids lived on the other side of the railroad tracks. They called it Little Italy.

Jackson's was an old-fashioned candy store owned by a brother and sister. It still had a Hershey's Ice Cream sign that hung above the wooden screen door, which was painted dark green along with the rest of the place. When my friends and I rode our bikes there in the summertime looking forward to an ice cream or candy, we always hoped Mr. Karl Jackson wasn't behind the counter! He made the Grinch look like a friendly guy. Instead, we hoped for his sister Becky. But, today, because I was with my dad, it didn't matter either way. Mr. Jackson was there behind the counter with his pipe clenched between his stained teeth. The pipe rested in the indentation that had formed in his lower lip from years of smoking it. I stood in front of the candy case, picking out all my favorite candies one by one. Tootsie Rolls, Mary Janes, Smarties, and Twisters were stuffed into a small brown paper bag just for me. Along with our candy, we bought six Fudgsicles and six Creamsicles for the family. I stood back while Mr. Jackson added up our purchase with a pencil and paper. He then used an old cash register to make a receipt. I watched his hand as it hit each button. He lost three of his fingers in the war, everybody said. It made him look even scarier. My older brother and his friends would tell stories at the dinner table of throwing change on the counter after they bought something, knowing that Mr. Jackson couldn't pick it up. My parents tried not to laugh, but Karl Jackson was such a grouch they would laugh and shake their heads. Dad slowly drove back up the mountain to give us time to enjoy our Fudgsicles before we got home.

CHAPTER 3: Flyboys

The first day of summer school was everything I expected;
it stunk. It was the same old math crap that hated me. Math just
hated my guts. It chewed me up and spit me out. The teacher
was a nice part-timer who seemed delighted to be there. It was
much to my bewilderment because all I could think about was
the whole summer passing me by outside. I think she thought

this class could really do it. Okay, so the upside was the cast of characters that made up my summer school class. For some reason, it was a bunch of boys and me. Most of them looked like they had been rolled around in the dirt against their will. They had messy hair, and their clothes looked like they were taken directly from the crumpled-up laundry pile freshly wrinkled! All of them except Jake made one too many left turns and were definitely headed in the wrong direction.

I understood I was different, in a good way, from the other kids in summer class, but a common denominator was that we all searched to find humor in everything because there was so much around us that was just hard. Jimmy was such a nut. He sat in the back wearing his olive green army jacket. It was long sleeved and came down over his hips. His hair was a nest of loose brown curls that needed to be cut. Today, he was busy nicknaming the three flies that had snuck into class when someone opened a door (or perhaps they made it through a tiny space between the screen and the windowsill). He wrote the names down on a piece of paper and passed it around the room. They were Hairy, Stinky, and Buzz. Buzz was the biggest fly, and Hairy, of course, was the hairiest. And I guess Stinky was named Stinky due to the fact that all flies spent time around things that stunk. As each day passed, the trio of fly mascots slowed down, losing the energy to menace the classroom. Lack of food and water was taking its toll on them. Unable to escape their huge jail cell, they croaked one by one. I loved animals, but flies did not make my A list, especially the green-headed flies and horseflies. Green-headed flies were aggressive, and horseflies would chase after you while trying to land for an opportunity to chomp on your flesh.

Jake had a big crush on me. He ran long distance and dreamed of making the cross-country track team. It was a big thing in our school. He sat next to me in class, and we giggled together at the other guys, never daring to pull the pranks but loving every minute of it!

Our first quiz yielded usual results for me: a big fat D+. When my mom picked me up after the first day of summer school, I just sat in the passenger seat with my shoulders hunched and my head down. I sat dejected with my quiz in my hands folded in half. Folding my papers in half was a habit I mindlessly took up when grades started to matter. My mom was my champion. "Don't give up! You're a winner! You need to practice and just keep trying," she insisted. "Okay," I said softly, although I felt in my heart that it was a lost cause.

CHAPTER 4: Museum Dog

After lunch, I enjoyed a Funnybone for dessert with a glass of cold milk over ice. There was a science to eating a Funnybone. First, I'd lick out the peanut butter and then bite off the chocolate shell, until all that remained was the chocolate sponge cake under my thumb and pointer finger. Once I got down to the chocolate sponge, I would alternate gulps of milk with bites of cake. I sat back in my chair, savoring the sugar high.

Mom announced it was front-page news: Mrs. Poole's dog was missing! "What?!" I screamed. There was a picture of the lost dog in the paper. I expected to see Mingpoo's fluffy head and the tiny pink bow on top of it in the photo. "What type of dog is that, Mom?" I asked as I leaned over her shoulder. Instead of a photo, it was a portrait of a dog, similar to those oil paintings you see in a museum. "What's its name, Mom?" "It doesn't say, Sammie," Mom said. "What? How can it not have a name? That's stupid!"

"Sammie, calm down. Mrs. Poole is an eccentric woman who does out-of-the-ordinary things. It says here in the paper that owner Theodora Poole will not reveal the name of the dog and gave no reason for her refusal not to do so. Instead, she offers a $10,000 reward for its safe return."

"Mom, the dog has to have a name!" "Sammie, go outside and play. Better still, don't you have to study?" Before I headed into the woods, I went into my dad's office and found a book on dog breeds located in the cabinet of his bookshelf. I turned each page slowly, looking at the pictures and reading the descriptions of each dog breed. Halfway through the book, I came across a picture of a dog that looked very similar to the one in the newspaper. The coloring wasn't the same, but everything else was. It read, "The Whippet is part of the sight hound family of dogs. They are bred to race and hunt small animals. Their bodies are lean and built for speed. An adult dog can run 35 to 40 mph. A Whippet does not bark, but it can let you know what it needs by observing its many expressions."

The remainder of the day I stayed in the woods, trying to get lost in some of my usual thoughts of great things I'm capable of doing. But, today, I couldn't do it. Instead, I sat down on a log next to the variety of bamboo plants that old lady Stein planted over 20 years ago, and I cried. We purchased some land from her and inherited the cool plants and trees from all over the world that she nurtured in happier times. Now she was our neighbor to the right and often chased after us dressed in a fuzzy pink sweater and clicking high heels. We never trespassed, but she would yell, "Get off my property, or I'll call the police!"

"Why is it so damn hard?" I asked, feeling sorry for myself and still crying. "I don't get it! I just want to run away. I want to be a jungle guide or something special."

I picked up a stick and started slashing at the tall bamboo stalks. My stick was a razor-sharp machete. My wiry arms were strong and able to cut back a path for me to move forward into the thickest part of the forest. I slashed through the stalks like I was a naturalist leading a grateful group of tourists deep into the wild. Before long, they were in awe of the wonders of the wilderness and looked at me with speechless adoration.

And then I saw it! Ahhh...it was wet and so sticky looking, jet black with two dark eyes! I've never seen a spider like this one. It was behind my favorite cluster of trees, the birch trees. I loved to peel the gray-white bark back and make miniature cones for the Native American tribe that adopted me in one of my many fantasies. I leaned forward to get a better look. I think it was a black widow spider? Wait a minute. That is impossible! Holy shoot, it could be a mutation! Move very slowly, I told myself. The black widow spider bites, and a giant one could kill someone! It moves and shakes the underbrush with a noise too big to be a spider. A head formed around what I now distinguished was a black nose. I screamed and fell back. It was a dog nose? I knew all the dog breeds. The sight hounds, the working group, the toy group, you name it. I was on it. But…I didn't recognize this dog. It moved toward me without a sound. Its ears were back over its narrow head, not signaling aggression but more like a curiosity. Its nose was now a few inches away from mine. Its slender foreleg rose up gracefully, and it rested its paw on top of my shoulder. It licked my nose. It was a dog.

"Wow," I whispered to myself. "What type of dog are you?" I asked it. It looked at me, head tilted. "Are you a boy or a girl?" I checked and saw that it was a boy. It was funny because the dog looked more like a girl. "Would it be okay, dog, if I looked at your tag?" I said out loud. "Are you going to bite me?" The dog took his paw off of my shoulder and stood very still, looking directly into my face. His eyes were soft and gentle, so I think it was safe to check. I carefully reached for his jeweled dog tag and turned it around to read what his name is. "Your name is Gage." With the sound of his name, the dog stepped into the nest that my crisscrossed legs created and turned around a few times. Still standing, Gage leaned up against me, wanting to be stroked. He was the softest dog I've ever touched. His coat was buttery soft and smelled like fresh raindrops. The background of his fur was white with tiger-like stripes of black and tan around his head, back, and bottom. His tail was so narrow you could see the tiny vertebrae. It tucked under his bottom, curling up at the end. His narrow snout was in perfect symmetry with his pin-shaped head and long, lean body. His ears were the only noticeably big detail. Everything else about Gage looked perfect. He wanted more affection, so I pet him wherever it appeared to feel good. I noticed how lightweight his fur was, and in some places I could see his skin. Around his slender legs and delicate elbows, the pink of his skin came through, and the blood was visible as it pulsed through tiny blue veins. I massaged his neck and back. Because he was so slender, I wasn't sure how to properly pet him. I was reassured because his eyes were closed, and his body relaxed as he let out a long sigh. He lied down in my crossed legs like a fawn, not like a typical dog. He turned his head backward to reach and lick the tears that had rolled over my cheeks and came to a stop at my chin. My heart smiled.

"What are you doing here, Gage?" I asked. He rose from his relaxed position and started to walk up the path deeper into the woods. He looked back, and I followed. As we walked, the squirrels, birds, and groundhogs scampered, fluttered, and scurried about, avoiding us like unknown threat. I noticed how Gage paid no attention to the other animals. Gage didn't make a sound as they made noise trying to escape either up trees or down into holes. His paws seemed to not quite touch the ground, making it appear like he floated millimeters above the ground. I followed Gage to the old foundation. My dad had done a typical "guy thing," as my mom described it, by renting a bulldozer to knock down the remainder of an abandoned servant's house that rested on a hill in the woods behind our property. What remained was the old foundation, as we called it. It was truly a kid's natural play land. It came with partially destroyed brick walls and marble steps that now went nowhere. Large pieces of sheetrock were layered on top of each other, cascading downward and providing the roof for a manmade cave. Gage stopped at the top of the marble steps, looking over the landscape like a small wolf.

"Do you like it here, Gage?" I asked. "It's really different. I don't think there's anything like it in the whole town." I launched into my historical tour guide fantasy, describing to Gage what the origin of this place was. "You see, Gage, this was part of an old estate. Years ago, a really important family named Post owned all the property on the mountain. George B. Post was a famous architect. He built huge buildings like the New York Stock Exchange building. That's why streets are named things like Post Road and Post Lane, where we live. They planted the beautiful trees and unusual plants. This place was where servants lived so they could take care of the family's needs." I looked down, to see that Gage was staring up at me. "Should I go on?" I asked. He started to prance around like a toy horse, bouncing up and down with excitement. "Okay," I laughed, "I'll finish the story."

Gage and I explored the old foundation the whole day. I was the princess of the castle while Gage was my bravest knight. I made him dog armor from the thick vines that grew on the gigantic maple trees. It was really a collar of vines, but Gage let me slide it over his head and around his slender neck. I sent him on secret missions to discover the whereabouts of our enemies, the groundhogs. He trotted off with his armored collar of vines and came back without it, a sure sign that he had tangled with the enemy and escaped to provide me with top-secret information that would help me save my kingdom. We defeated the enemy together and celebrated the together. We won! I piled wild red raspberries and blackberries on a piece of smooth slate that I picked while Gage was on one of his missions. The slate stepping stone was part of the path that snaked around from the old foundation to Mrs. Stein's property line. I ate the berries while Gage dozed on his back, eyes closed, in the late afternoon sun. His dog belly was warm under my hand, and he dozed for a long time. The sun was low, and the horizon was pink with orange rays of color. Gage and I played all day, and it was coming to an end. He rolled over unto his feet and balanced on his hind legs, pushing his paws onto my tummy. He jumped off the foundation wall and began to trot down the path to the bamboo patch. He went to the edge and stood waiting for me to catch up.

"Gage, wait. Don't go back into the woods. Come home with me tonight. You can sleep with me. You must be hungry and thirsty. Please come. Don't leave me!" I pleaded. Gage shook his head. "Will you be here tomorrow after school? Please say yes. Please?" Gage bowed a playful puppy bow, and his lip furled up on one side, making an unmistakable dog smile. He turned into the bamboo and disappeared behind the birch tree.

CHAPTER 5: Discovery

I ran down the path and whipped into the laundry room. My sister said, "You look like you got attacked by wolves, stupid."

"Be quiet!" I shouted back.

"Girls!" my mother yelled from the hallway for us to stop. I took off my sneakers and jeans, wrapped a towel around me, and raced down the hallway to my bedroom to change for dinner. After dinner, I raided the pantry for pretzels, chips and grabbed the portable TV from the basement. There were no TVs in our bedrooms, which was good because I was addicted to cartoons and PBS. I loved the stories that aired on PBS. They were always about someone like the Count of Monte Cristo or Jane Eyre. They were the underdogs, fighting for freedom or for love! I climbed into bed with my snack mix and began to watch a movie. One of my favorites was on: The Magnificent Seven. It's about a good gang of cowboy gunslingers that band together to save a town that was being beaten up by bullies. About a quarter of the way into it, I saw a dog in the background of one scene barking at a horse. At that moment the realization came to me. I throw up my hands, knocking over my bowl of snacks and then grabbing it before it fell off the bed and woke everyone up!

Oh, God, the newspaper. You need to get the newspaper, I said to myself. Mom was watching TV in her room, and Dad was snoring on the recliner in the family room. I tiptoed out of my bedroom and down the hallway to the TV room where Dad was sleeping. The newspaper was motionless underneath the TV remote on the end table next to my Dad's chair. I walked on the balls of my feet like martial arts experts did in the movies. Silently, I moved across the floor to the edge of the table. Dad's chest rose up and down. He stopped breathing for a second and then snorted loudly to chase his breath. "Oh, please, let me get it," I said to myself. I lifted the remote and then the newspaper. My dad woke up! "Here, Sammie. You can watch something if you want. I'm going to bed," he said, much to my relief.

"Okay, Dad," I said, frozen. When I heard the door to my parents' bedroom shut, I took the newspaper back to my room and closed the door. I shut off the TV and began to turn the pages. I was trying to remember if it was on the second page of the paper...third page...there it was. Geez Louise. It's Gage! I threw my hand over my mouth in order to muffle my shock. Gage belonged to Mrs. Poole. He was the missing dog in the picture!

CHAPTER 6: The Long Wait

Paying attention in class was not an option for me the next day. God knows I needed to stay focused on the subject if I planned to pass, but all I could think about was Gage. I had so many questions about where he came from, why was he in my woods, what he wanted, and what type of dog he was. He was magical! There was no doubt, like something out of a storybook. Maybe I was destined to be a dog trainer or an animal psychic.

I don't remember climbing into our station wagon after school that day. I was in the passenger seat waiting impatiently to get home so I could see Gage. "What? I have to do what?" "You have to go to your friend Leslie's birthday party," my mother reminded me.

"It's a swim party?" I hesitated. I couldn't tell mom about Gage. Well, last year I sent out invitations to my swim birthday party. My mom and I selected April 15th. My birthday was actually the 19th of April. The 15th fell on a Saturday, so it worked great for a swim party. I was proud of myself for writing, addressing, and mailing the invitations. Unfortunately, Leslie's invitation said the 13th instead of the 15th. I was so embarrassed when she showed up with her mom, thinking the celebration was the 13th. It was one of those "I wish I could disappear" moments. Leslie was one of my smart friends. I was sure she thought I was stupid. I hoped a year later she had forgotten about my trouble with threes and fives.

The party was fun, and I got away without any mention of last year's blunder. It was dinnertime at my house, and you didn't miss it! No matter what, my parents always wanted the family to have dinner together. I ate very little and then faked a stomach ache. In my bed, I looked out the window toward the woods. My mom checked on me one more time before she went to bed. I slid from underneath the covers, climbed out my bedroom window with my flashlight, and dropped to the ground like a cougar. The moon was full, so it was easy to see the path from my house to the woods. Not needing the flashlight, I left it in the bushes. I sprinted up the path to the bamboo patch and cluster of birch trees, I stopped and waited.

"Gage," I said softly and a little out of breath. "It's me, Sammie," I said. Gage appeared from behind the birch tree. The moonlight washed over his coat, illuminating the white in his fur. He looked like he was glowing. We greeted each other with enthusiasm. Gage looked at me and then at the moon.

"What is it, Gage?" I asked. "Do you want to tell me why you ran away from Mrs. Poole? She has to be mean because she never says hello." Gage walked across the path to the oak tree and sniffed the old acorns that rested at the bottom. Most of them had been picked over by the squirrels, but he was able to find ones he liked. Gage picked the last of the whole ones up, one at a time in his mouth balancing each one on the long log. Next, he stood and looked at me and then at the log. I sat down on the end of the log, staring at the acorns.

"So, what is this, Gage? What do you want me to do with 10 acorns?" Gage jumped over the log and back again, back and forth, back and forth over the log. He jumped so high I stood up and clapped. Gage then removed five of them one by one, careful not to damage them with his teeth.

"So, now there are five?" Gage looked into my eyes. "Are you trying to teach me math? Oh my God. Are you kidding me? You know how to do math? How can that be? This is ridiculous!" He looked at the moon and turned toward the bamboo. He looked over his shoulder at me and then he disappeared. I didn't protest by asking him to stay with me. It was late now, and I had school tomorrow. I sat for a few minutes thinking about what just happened before I went back home.

CHAPTER 7: On a Mission

As soon as I got home from school, I took my knapsack, math book, pencil, and calculator with me as I burst through the side door of our house. Racing past the cranberry tree and patches of wild blackberries, I jumped on top of the long log and sat down outside the bamboo patch.

"Gage, where are you?' I called. Gage appeared, and at the sight of my math book he put his ears back, smiled, and started to spin around in a circle. He was spinning so fast he was a blur of colors. He looked like a speckled tornado, stopping and then going in the opposite direction. When he spun around for the last time, he had carved out a hole in the dirt that was a foot deep. He looked up at me and I burst out laughing; I fell on the ground cracking up at the sight of him. He sprung out of the hole like a gazelle and landed on me, licking and nuzzling my face.

"Wow, Gage! You're nuts! So, are you going to teach me today?" I asked in a quiet voice. I was convinced Gage could answer all my hopes to be a normal girl, not different. We walked to the green Japanese maple tree. I sat on a branch, and Gage lay down on the long grass where a deer had made a bed the night before. Looking up at me, he tilted his head.

"So," I said, "are you going to help me?" I waited, but Gage just lay there with his head on top of his front paws. He blinked his brown eyes in between long stares.

"Gage, I have to study, and I thought that you were going to teach me how to do this stuff. We had a second quiz, you know, and I got another D+. I'm going to fail if someone doesn't help me. I can't do it myself. You're smart. You can help me!" I started to feel desperately frustrated. It was so easy for me to go from happy to complete frustration.

"What am I going to do? I have a quiz on Friday that I need to pass! I know you understand me, Gage. Don't just lie there and stare at me!" He lifted his head and stood up. His eyes were wet and sad. He turned away and started a slow and deliberate trot back down the path.

"Where are you going?" I yelled after him. Trailing behind him, I could see his narrow tail was tucked tighter than normal under his slender body. The top of his head was not visible from behind; it hung low.

"Gage, please, I'm sorry if I yelled..." I ran after him, but he was already at the birch tree, and gone. I was frantic! What was I going to do now? I had no one I could confide in about what just happened. Come on. A dog that could do what Gage was capable of doing? Now I was sure he was a lost dog. On top of that, he belonged to Mrs. Poole! Mom said that Mrs. Demarco told her that Mrs. Poole parked her luxury convertible in her living room. So, if her living room was her garage, where did she sleep, and where did Gage sleep? I didn't want him to go back to her. Even if I told someone, Gage would not have anything to do with me anymore! I retreated deep into the woods where the Big Hill was. A huge cherry tree was planted long ago and halfway down the hill. It was 80 feet high, with tiny white blossoms hanging from its branches. The branches hung low over the Big Hill, arching from one side to the other, forming a tunnel over the downhill path. My older brother had tied a knot in the end of a thick rope and through it over the lowest branch of the tree, making an instant swing! I remember how amazed I was that a piece of rope could become a swing in a matter of minutes. I would swing way up high and then jump off the rope and land on the hill, rolling the rest of the way down. As I rolled over and over, I imagined I was the first female stuntwoman ever to conquer the Big Hill after jumping from a rope swing! I was a daredevil like no one had ever seen. But today, I didn't feel like a daredevil. I straddled the rope and swung around in small circles, pushing off the ground with the tip of my toe when my momentum slowed.

"How would I think that a dog, even a magical one, could teach me anything?" I said to the ground. I began to cry. I said out loud what I thought was the truth: that it would take magic to get me to pass summer school. What will happen to me now? I hugged myself as I swung. I was lost.

CHAPTER 8: A School Day

Jake asked me to the movies while we sat learning Algebra. "What's playing?" I mumbled. We both loved science fiction, so he had chosen the latest sci-fi movie and picked a show time for this Friday. I absently said sure. Shortly after, Buzz the fly came into my trance-like view. He looked like a small plane pulling one of those paid advertisements that you saw when you went to the beach. They would fly low over the ocean, proclaiming, "Drink specials at the Tiki Bar tonight starting at 5:00!" Only Buzz was pulling a piece of thread. Jimmy had tied it to his fly body and then let him go. He climbed high then down again, moving slowly across the classroom. We all cracked up! Our stomachs cramped with laughter. Even our nice part-time teacher could not hold back her amusement. She let us have a short break but not too long because we had a lot to cover.

"Hey, Jimmy. Why don't you use your powers for good instead of evil?" one kid said to him as we hung out in the hallway around the soda machine. I guzzled a Coke, letting the sugar soak into my veins, energizing my imagination.

"Shut up," Jimmy said to the kid. He looked especially scruffy today. I asked him how he tied the thread to the fly, and he said he talked to the fly and asked it to stand still.

"Yeah, right Jimmy so you're a fly tamer," I said smugly. Jimmy just laughed and went outside to sneak a cigarette. Danny Shelton chimed in, "Hey, Sammie! Why don't you go back across the tracks to Little Italy where you belong with the rest of the Italians?" "I don't live over the railroad tracks, idiot," I snapped back at him.

I was thankful for Jake today because we spent the rest of class whispering about all of the different sci-fi fly scenarios we could think about. The best one was the mutant fly spitting acid saliva all over the school and melting everyone inside. Of course, the fly looking for revenge was Buzz. He was determined to find Jimmy in the sea of humans running and screaming as they tried to escape the horrible scene. Finally, it found Jimmy, running across the football field with a cigarette hanging from his mouth. Buzz got him as he was climbing the fence that encircled the field. The only thing left of Jimmy was a smoldering cigarette lying on the ground.

CHAPTER 9: Making Things Right Again

It was Saturday, and I could hear Mom answer the phone while I changed into my shorts from my jeans, not sure what I was doing. It was my friend Nancy. Nancy and I were some of the best runners in school. Sprinters, to be specific. We were both destined for the track team. The high school track coach had already poked his head into our gym class while we ran relay races and played dodge ball, smiling at our quickness he asked us to get excited about high school track and field.

Nancy's entire family of six kids was comprised of A students. One day during the school year I didn't realize that I had forgotten my math book in my locker. I climbed on the bus sitting across from Nancy. She noticed it was missing because I had let her know I had a quiz coming up. She asked where my math book was. I said I guess I forgot it. She suggested I ask the driver to stop the bus so I could run back for my math book. I sheepishly said no and that I would have my mom drive me back to pick it up. I didn't want to embarrass myself in front of everyone on the bus. Nancy was one of my only friends who knew I was not a good student. I'm sure she thought it was because I did things like leave my math book in my locker and didn't study hard enough. I hated that she didn't really understand how hard I tried in school because school was so easy for her. But she was my best friend and liked me anyway. Today, Nancy wanted to know if I was up for our usual bike ride to Rattle Snake Road. There was a huge horse farm on the corner, which was about 10 miles one way from my house. We had to go down Jacobs Ladder, which was an area of road that was fun to go down, but coming up was a challenge. It was really steep with deep step-like indentations. In the old days, my dad explained that the steps in the ladder allowed the horse and carriages to stop and rest before finally getting to the top. Each time Nancy and I got to the top we would talk about how awesome it was that we could ride up Jacobs Ladder without stopping. However, today I didn't want to go. I asked my mom to tell Nancy that I needed to study, an idea that both mom and Nancy agreed with.

Dad was working on the property like he did every Saturday, and I was his helper. It was hard to concentrate on yardwork when I wanted to make things right again with Gage.

"Sammie, get the electric hedge trimmer from the tool shed and start on the bushes in the front." As I worked, Dad complained, "The darn deer eat everything. As soon as a flower pops its head above the ground, the deer gobble it up! I should get my 22-caliber and just shoot the stupid things." "Dad, they need to eat," I said, defending the deer. "What is this?" my dad asked.

"Looks like a flashlight?" I said with a question. I had forgotten I left it in the bushes the night I snuck out my bedroom window to see Gage. Thank God for an interruption.

"Sir, Sir!" Dad and I both turned around at the same time. There was a woman on the other side of the wrought-iron fence that surrounded our property. "Sir, please come here and help this poor deer!" My dad walked over to the inside of the fence, and I followed. The woman on the other side was Mrs. Poole. Her black and gray hair was pulled into a familiar bun, and she was wearing a black dress. The dress had a single piece of jewelry on it: a jeweled pin on the collar, like something you saw on a famous movie actress. The pin was encrusted with diamonds and sapphires. It was so big I could see the jewels from where I was standing, which was about 50 feet behind my dad. She had on a fur coat, which was strange because it was summertime.

"Sammie," my dad yelled over his shoulder, "go get the crow bar!" I ran like a bullet back to the tool shed and pulled the crow bar off the shed wall. As I ran back, I wanted to ask Mrs. Poole about Gage. Why did he run away? Did he run away because she was mean to him? Did she keep him in the living room with her car? I dashed back over the lawn, past the pool deck, and back to where my dad was waiting. A deer had raced across the road in a panic and got its head stuck in the fence. In order to free it, Dad put the crow bar through the fence. Next, he put his hand on the deer's head, and Mrs. Poole quickly asked him to be careful not to hurt the deer. I couldn't help but look at her face. Her mouth was small, and she had the bluest eyes I'd ever seen. They were a dark shade of blue, which made her eyes look black at first glance. Her legs were long and slender, pale against her black dress. She looked like a model from Vogue magazine, although she was older and didn't smile.

"I won't hurt it," Dad said. "Just stand back, Theodora." Mrs. Poole took a step back as Dad pried the bars apart. At the same time, he pushed the deer's head back. It was finally free and quickly galloped across the road crossing Mrs. Poole's apple orchard, disappearing into the trees. "Oh, thank you, sir," she said, wiping at her eyes with a handkerchief embroidered with the initials TP. When she opened her car door, I could see a small pillow on the passenger seat that had Mingpoo's picture sewn into the material. Mrs. Poole gracefully slid onto the leather seat of her convertible and drove home. As we walked back toward the house, Mom came out to see what happened. "A deer got its head stuck in the fence, Mom!" I shouted. "After all these years of living here, she kept calling me Sir," my dad said, annoyed. "Hey, Dad, the bushes are done. Can I go play?" Dad was preoccupied with thoughts of Mrs. Poole and answered absently, "Sure, Sammie."

I put gas in my Honda 50 motorcycle and drove up the path to the woods. I picked some of my favorite violet-colored wildflowers. They were tiny, delicate flowers that grew low to the ground. I placed them near the foot of the birch tree and then put the bike in first gear, driving slowly up and to the left of the path. I sat on the lowest branch of the tree fort, thinking about the acorns that Gage had gathered when, all of a sudden, I felt the soft fur of his face on my neck. I turned to see him, with the flowers in his collar. "I'm sorry, Gage," I said.

CHAPTER 10: Amazing

Gage and I spent the day in the tree fort. My cousins and I built it last summer. It wasn't a tree house. Instead, we created steps by nailing two by fours into alternating branches. This way we could climb the tree to the upper branches and defend our fort from our older cousins who wanted to destroy us. It wasn't the tallest tree; it was a green maple tree, with branches that grew wider instead of higher and leaves shaped like snowflakes. Its shape made climbing easier, and still the highest branches made for a great lookout. On the upper branches, we nailed plywood boards that acted like seats. I sometimes felt bad hammering nails into the branches of the tree. My mom explained it was like getting a cut on your knee and not having a bandage to put over to make sure it healed. I guess my need for a tree fort was more important than letting insects into the tree's branches. As I hammered each nail in, I told the tree that I was sorry. The highest board was on a branch that extended out over the path. It was the lookout station. In history class we learned all about the Revolutionary War. George Washington would have made me his right-hand officer if he could see how well I could defend my tree fort from the enemy.

I could see for a mile on a clear day from the lookout perch. It was my responsibility to protect the fort while the troops marched to the old foundation to fight the enemy. With the troops gone, it was up to Gage and I to protect the fort from enemy spies sent to destroy it.

"Okay, Gage. We have to make weapons to defend ourselves." Gage looked at me, interested. "We need to make swords for one-on-one combat and cannonballs to launch at spies to keep them from crossing into our territory." Gage trotted away and came back with long sticks cleaned of their small branches. Gage was a great climber. He was up on the lookout perch with me. I used the pocketknife that my Dad gave me to make a sharp point at the end for each stick that Gage had collected. Gage looked over my shoulder while I worked hard to make something that looked like a sword. It took us hours to prepare the fort for the future attack. Gage carried stones from the gravel dump to act as cannonballs. Each one was a palm size stone, identical to each other. As I worked, I told Gage how great it was to see things from up high.

"Gage," I said, "you are totally the king of the world up here. Nothing bothers you. I wish I could stay up here forever." Gage listened intently like he always did. "Gage, why did you run away from Mrs. Poole's place?" With that, Gage scurried down the tree, jumping from board to board, and landed on the ground with a soft whisper. He looked up at me and walked backwards and then up on his hind legs for me to follow.

"Gage," I yelled down, "we're almost done filling the arsenal with weapons! We can't quit now! What if we get attacked?" Gage kept walking backwards. "Okay," I said, "here I come!" I swung off the branch that extended over the path and hit the ground.

Gage exploded with speed. The open field was just up ahead and around the corner. I took a few running steps and saw that he was already out of view. Quickly, I hopped on my motorcycle and raced through the gears, first, second, third, and finally forth. I turned the corner, full speed now, and saw Gage racing like a thoroughbred horse toward the field. He was so fast my eyes strained to track him. I was pushing the Honda to 50 mph and couldn't catch him! Then, something amazing happened: Gage lifted into the air. His long forelegs were stretched out in front of him, guiding the direction of his flight. His ears were tucked back, making him less resistant to the air, which moved efficiently over his sleek body. He circled around toward me, and I could see his eyes were slightly closed to protect them from the rushing wind. Gage was a flying dog! My mouth was wide open, which I didn't realize until a felt a tickle of saliva flow over the corner of my mouth. I caught it with my hand and wiped it on my shorts. Gage circled in the sky again and then came down to the ground, walking as he landed, hardly making a sound.

I stepped off my bike and collapsed onto both knees. My eyes watered from what I saw Gage do. "How can this be?" I said out loud, "I..." Gage trotted over to me and nudged my shoulder with his snout. I was off balance, and his gentle push knocked me on my side. I caught myself with my hand and stayed in that position for a few seconds until Gage pawed at the top of my shoulder. I slowly got up, not sure what was happening. He walked to the top of the hill overlooking the field. There he stopped, looking out over the scenery and past it to the beautiful trees that dotted the landscape. They were all in some stage of bloom. Full and round with colorful blossoms, it was a beautiful picture painted for the world to see. I walked over and stood next to him. He looked like a hieroglyphic of those ancient dogs that you see in history books. I think it was Egypt, but I wasn't sure.

I looked out over the woods and saw things I never noticed before. I thought I knew everything about these woods. Every cool place was my personal discovery. It was my private world to wander around in. I closed my eyes for a long time. I began to smell new scents. The honeysuckle was sweet and filled my nostrils with fragrance. The birds were singing as usual, but now I could hear that each one had a distinct song. At this moment, the woodpecker caught my ear. I opened my eyes and followed the sound like radar. I spotted him high up on a tree, pecking a hole with his brilliant red head. I felt like I could see and hear so many things for the first time, like nothing missed my senses. I'm felt sure I was floating, but the ground was under my feet. I felt full of something amazing. Gage was close by because I could feel him next to my leg. His dog body was warm and radiated a comforting heat. Suddenly, I was exhausted, hungry, and thirsty. Gage sensed my needs and turned away from the field, moving toward the path. I straddled my dirt bike and started the engine. Together, we started for home, me on my bike and Gage walking alongside me. I braked at the bamboo patch. "I guess you're here because you weren't happy living with Mrs. Poole. I think you wanted to run and maybe she kept you in the house all the time?" He looked at me with a determined expression, and then he disappeared behind the birch tree. I rode to the tool shed to put my bike away.

At the dinner table, different thoughts occupied my mind. I wasn't thinking about school tomorrow. Instead, I asked my mom how she made eggplant that tasted so delicious. My dad was sharing his day with us like he always did: how he saved money and negotiated a deal.

"Save your money, kid. You never know when you'll need it," he advised me. I got up to get another plate of food, and he grabbed the tail of my t-shirt and tugged on it. I was a human yo-yo. We both laughed at how I tried to make it back to my seat with a full dinner plate in my hand. He pushed and pulled me back and forth. I spun toward him and then away from him, much to my mother's protest. "Be careful," she warned my dad, "she has a plate in her hand."

"Come on, Dad. Tell me how to save money. How do I do it right?" I asked. I sat down and listened while inhaling food.

"Well, there's something called compounded interest. It's very simple. You put money in your savings account. The bank gives you interest, or a percentage on your savings. Each month the interest is calculated on the amount of money in the account. With each passing month, the percentage is calculated on the amount plus the previous month's interest. It keeps building and building, just like a bird building a nest. The bird layers the sticks one on top of another, and the nest gets larger until it's ready for the eggs. Do you understand, Sammie?"

"Yeah, I get it," I said. "I want to have a lot of money someday, so I'm going to put it into a savings account. I'm going to sell lemonade all summer, too!" "That's the way, Sammie!" Dad said. "Act like a squirrel, and store your nuts away for the wintertime." We stayed at the dinner table until the summer sun finally set. It was 8:00 pm when the last dish was put away. My eyes were so heavy all I could think about now was getting into bed and sleep. "Mom, do you really think I can pass summer school? Because I don't think I can do it," I asked my mom as I brushed my teeth and got ready for bed.

"Sammie, I think you can do anything you put your mind to," Mom said, "but class isn't until Monday, and you have Sunday night to get ready for your quiz on Monday. Don't worry about it. Go to sleep." I looked at myself in the mirror and saw my green eyes against my tanned face and dark hair. Normally, my reflection would remind me that I looked like an aunt that everyone complained about. Tonight, the girl in the mirror looked different. I guess I looked kind of...pretty?

I was tired like I never felt before. It was like every bone in my body was exhausted. The sheets in my bed were cool next to my sun-soaked limbs and face. I fell into a deep sleep. Gage was in my dreams that night. I was asking him how I could fly. He kept taking me back to the acorns, sitting on the log trying to show me something. I stood there by the long log and stared at the acorns. I heard the eagle cry overhead. It was diving hard at something. Its eyes were fierce and bright like yellow flames. It was coming at me with all its speed and intensity. I stepped onto the long log to face it. I squared off my body and braced myself for the impact. My back was wet with sweat; my eyes gleamed, never blinking. The acorns flew off the log as I jumped up to catch the bird. It barreled into my body, and I held onto it as I fell backward. I landed softly against the earth. The eagle faded away in my arms.

CHAPTER 11: A New Day

I woke up Sunday morning with scratches on my arms. I couldn't remember where they came from. I always felt a bruise or saw a scratch after the fact. It wasn't unusual because I was always caught up in the moment. Did I scratch them jumping from the tree fort? No…it was the dream I remembered. I walked out to the kitchen. "How would you like your eggs, Sammie?" Mom asked.

"Ah…scrambled, I guess." I walked past my mother and to the medicine cabinet in the kitchen. I wasn't tall enough to reach it, so I had to kneel on the counter to find the Band-Aids and anti-bacteria ointment. "What did you do?" Mom asked, alarmed. I looked down and saw the deep scratches again. I tried to downplay them. "Oh, it's fine. I just tripped and fell into the sticker bushes. It's not that bad, Mom." "Sammie," Mom warned, "you have to be more careful in the woods. Please don't stay up there all day today. Grandma and Grandpa are coming for lunch, so come down around 1:00, do you hear me?" "Yes," I replied. "By the way, shouldn't you be studying today?" Mom asked. "Yeah, I'm going to, Mom," I said. I gathered up all my quizzes, math book, sharpened pencils, calculator, and paper and put them in my knapsack. Cheese corn chips, soda, and Tootsie Rolls went into the side pockets. I was on a mission. I rolled out the Honda, started the engine, and rode into the woods.

Upon setting my bike down, I called for Gage. "Hey, Gage!" I said, "Let's count some acorns today!" Gage popped his head out from behind the bamboo stalks, nose first. It reminded of the first day I discovered him. I thought his nose was a poisonous spider! I sat down on the log, and Gage made a bed for himself in the tall grass that grew in front. He was curled into a tight ball, with his head resting across his body. He listened while I reviewed the chapters and retook the tests. Each time it got a little better. I could unscramble more of the mystery that was the math puzzle.

"All I want, Gage, is a C+," I said with a smile. "No use trying to bite off more than you can chew! Speaking of that," I reached into my knapsack for some chips and soda, "let's take a break now. It's almost 1:00, and my brain hurts." We lay down for a while together. I crunched my chips, washing them down with soda while Gage gnawed on a stick.

"Sammie!" Mom yelled out for me to come down for lunch. "Grandma and Grandpa are here. Come on down!" I put my school stuff back in my knapsack and the garbage into the plastic bag I brought. Gage got up and came over to me. He buried his head in my body and then put his paws on my shoulders as I knelt down in front of him. It felt like he was hugging me.

"I made a mistake, Gage," I said. "I thought I discovered you, but you were the one that found me." I started to cry. Not because I felt sorry for myself, but because I knew I wouldn't see Gage again and would miss him. He would always be in my heart. I knew it was important to him to understand that I would always love him. He licked my tears. I stood up, threw my knapsack over my shoulder, and climbed on my bike. Gage stood in front of the birch tree. Then, he was gone.

CHAPTER 12: Flying High

My dad picked me up from summer school today. "Hey, champ. How did you do on your last day of school?" He said with enthusiasm. "It's your last day Sammie, freedom, freee... dom, baby!" he said, laughing. "Okay, Dad," I said. "So, did you pass or fail?" he asked. "I don't know yet," I lied. I told a lie knowing that I would later tell the truth. I called them bridge lies.

They bought you time before you had to tell the truth, and they were only acceptable to tell when the truth was good news, never the other way around. The truth was, the teacher gave the class their final exams back today. It was in my knapsack. As soon as dad put the car in park I opened the car door, jumped out of the car, and raced up the path to the woods.

"Where are you going?" Dad called after me. "We're going to eat lunch now!" I knew when my Dad was serious and when he was getting a kick out of his daughter, so I kept on running and shouted back over my shoulder, "I'll be right down. I have something to do!" I grinned from ear to ear as I turned and ran around the pretty maple tree, raced past the old foundation, and made a sharp left turn at the place where the deer slept. I jumped onto the floor of the gazebo, which was surrounded by beautiful peonies. Peonies smelled like nice perfume, not old lady perfume that you sometimes smelled while walking around the mall. The smell was fresh and beautiful. The blossoms were a combination of light pink with darker pink edges. The flowers had layer upon layer of soft petals. I picked a great big bouquet, which I briefly admired. "Mom will love these," I thought out loud.

I took the long way home by walking back over the path I had raced up a few moments ago. I walked past the place where the deer slept and the old foundation. I crossed over to the rope swing, which swayed over the big hill while being pushed by a summer breeze. Then, I made my way around the green maple tree and past the bamboo patch. I picked some wild violets and placed them on the tall grass near the long log. I could see my house now. My family was outside on the screened-in porch. The grill smoked, and the smell of chicken and sausage cooking filled the air. It was a picture I would look forward to every weekend from now on. I couldn't wait to get home!

In my hurry to join my family, the tip of my sneaker hit the root of the big pine tree. I stumbled, and fell to one knee. My bouquet of flowers gently plopped beside me, cradled by the long grass. As I went to pick up the flowers, I looked over my shoulder at the bamboo patch. Gage was there. He looked very regal and intelligent, with his front legs on the long log and his head straight and high. He smiled at me, and I grinned back at him before I got up and ran toward the house.

"Hi, Mom. These flowers are for you!" She spun around from the sink and asked, "Where did you get them? They're beautiful!" "They're peonies," I said, proudly. "What's the occasion?" Mom asked. "I got a C+ on my final math exam!" I said, smiling. "Hey, kid. I knew you could do it!" Dad said as he entered the kitchen. "I'm so proud of you, Sammie," Mom said with a tear. I was so happy I couldn't stop laughing! We all laughed together.

Escaping to the woods was not as appealing as it was just a few days ago. Don't get me wrong. It was a great place to walk and think, but it had become a part of the rest of my summer and was no longer my entire world. I often think about Gage and how I loved him for the lessons he taught me. The most important one was to have faith in myself. I always wanted to fly like an eagle so I could achieve great things. In my heart, I knew now that I was already flying high in the sky, looking down on all of life's challenges and the unbelievable good stuff.

CHAPTER 13: The Right Thing

The following Sunday my grandparents arrived. I ran
outside to help them with the groceries. My grandma sent me
out to pick dandelion leaves to make a salad. We ate lunch and
then spent the rest of the day relaxing around the pool. I did
more relaxing than swimming today. I read the Sunday comics,
Parade Magazine, and the advice column. I chatted with my

friends on the phone and planned to have three of them over on Monday for a swim.

"Sammie," Mom said from inside the porch. "You would be interested in knowing that Mrs. Poole found her lost dog." I got up and walked over to the screen to see the newspaper. Mom tilted the page my way so I could see the article, which was printed with the same painting of Gage. This time the headline read, "Dog of regal lineage takes rightful place in owner's home."

"Can I read it, Mom?" "Sure, Sammie. Here's the article," Mom said, sliding the section out of the newspaper out for me. I opened the door and reached in to take it from her. I brought it over to my beach towel, sat down, and read it aloud to myself.

EPILOGUE

There will be no reward for a Good Samaritan for the safe return of a dog belonging to Theodora Poole, of 13 Claremont Road, Bernardsville, NJ. Police say that Mrs. Poole called the department late last Sunday night, demanding that they conduct an investigation into who had stolen her Whippet. "She was very upset," said Officer Ryan Kirk. According to the officer's report, there is now good news, Mrs. Poole found the dog, named "Karajan's Granted Wish," on her doorstep with a collar of tiny violet flowers around its neck. A sure sign, she said, that someone had taken and kept the dog. It turns out the lost dog was a Whippet descended from a long line of award-winning show dogs. Mrs. Poole did not reveal these details in the initial report for fear that someone would hold the dog for ransom.

"Mrs. Poole was emotional due to the fact that her 12-year-old Pekingese had to be put to sleep approximately one week ago," Officer Kirk said. Mrs. Poole had kept the lost dog at her summer home due to the fact that the breed does better in more moderate climates. She brought it to her home in Bernardsville on a temporary basis while she was preparing to leave for her summer home.

"The case will probably never be explained, but we are happy that the dog is back safe and sound," Officer Kirk concluded.

CPSIA information can be obtained
at www.ICGtesting.com
Printed in the USA
BVOW09s0316030717

488380BV00001B/31/P